Dear Parent:

Congratulations! Your child is taking the first steps on an exciting journey. The destination? Independent reading!

STEP INTO READING® will help your child get there. The program offers five steps to reading success. Each step includes fun stories and colorful art. There are also Step into Reading Sticker Books, Step into Reading Math Readers, Step into Reading Phonics Readers, Step into Reading Write-In Readers, and Step into Reading Phonics Boxed Sets—a complete literacy program with something to interest every child.

Learning to Read, Step by Step!

Ready to Read   Preschool–Kindergarten
• big type and easy words • rhyme and rhythm • picture clues
For children who know the alphabet and are eager to begin reading.

Reading with Help   Preschool–Grade 1
• basic vocabulary • short sentences • simple stories
For children who recognize familiar words and sound out new words with help.

Reading on Your Own   Grades 1–3
• engaging characters • easy-to-follow plots • popular topics
For children who are ready to read on their own.

Reading Paragraphs   Grades 2–3
• challenging vocabulary • short paragraphs • exciting stories
For newly independent readers who read simple sentences with confidence.

Ready for Chapters   Grades 2–4
• chapters • longer paragraphs • full-color art
For children who want to take the plunge into chapter books but still like colorful pictures.

STEP INTO READING® is designed to give every child a successful reading experience. The grade levels are only guides. Children can progress through the steps at their own speed, developing confidence in their reading, no matter what their grade.

Remember, a lifetime love of reading starts with a single step!

For Kelly and Sean,
who are good friends
most of the time —M.W.

To Graham —S.B.

Text copyright © 2012 by Melissa Wiley
Cover art and interior illustrations copyright © 2012 by Sebastien Braun

Step into Reading, Random House, and the Random House colophon are registered trademarks of Random House, Inc.

Visit us on the Web!
StepIntoReading.com
randomhouse.com/kids

Educators and librarians, for a variety of teaching tools, visit us at
randomhouse.com/teachers

Library of Congress Cataloging-in-Publication Data
Wiley, Melissa.
Fox and Crow are not friends / by Melissa Wiley ; illustrated by Sebastien Braun.
  p. cm. — (Step into reading. Step 3)
Summary: Continuing Aesop's fable, Fox and Crow tussle over pieces of cheese, but Mama, one of the three bears, outwits them both.
ISBN 978-0-375-86982-2 (trade) — ISBN 978-0-375-96982-9 (lib. bdg.) —
ISBN 978-0-375-98574-4 (ebook)
[1. Foxes—Fiction. 2. Crows—Fiction. 3. Bears—Fiction. 4. Characters in literature—Fiction.]
I. Braun, Sebastien, ill. II. Title.
PZ7.W64814Fox 2012 [E]—dc23 2011043350

Printed in the United States of America
10 9 8 7 6 5 4 3 2 1

STEP INTO READING®

STEP 3

Fox and Crow Are **NOT** Friends

by Melissa Wiley

illustrated by Sebastien Braun

Random House New York

Chapter 1

A Nice Bit of Cheese

Fox and Crow

did not like each other one bit.

You might have heard

about their very first fight.

It started over a piece of cheese.

Crow found it first.

She flew to a tree to eat it.

Fox spotted

the big hunk of cheese.

He loved a nice bit of cheese.

Crow was about to gulp it down.

Fox had to act fast.

"Hello, Crow!"

he called.

"How are you on this fine day?"

Crow did not answer.

Fox tried again.

"How fine you look

up there in that tree!

Your feathers shine

in the sun.

You make the sky

look more blue.

What a lovely bird you are!"

Crow was pleased.

She gave her wings a proud flap.

Still, she did not answer.

Fox tried again.

"I bet your song is

as fine as your feathers.

I would love to hear you sing!"

Crow could not resist.

She opened her beak and sang.

"Caw! Caw! Caw!"

The cheese tumbled down.

11

It fell right into Fox's mouth.

He gobbled it up, lickety-split.

He licked his lips and laughed.

Crow glared at Fox.

"You had better watch out, Fox,"

she said.

"You may be a sly fox,

but crows are very smart.

You took my cheese.

I will get even with you!"

"You don't scare me, Crow,"
said Fox.
Crow dived at Fox,
but Fox ran into the bushes.
From that day on,
Fox and Crow were enemies.

Chapter 2

A Good Smell Is Hard to Find

Crow had a plan.

The plan needed three things—

a piece of string,

a piece of cheese,

and a good smell.

The string was easy to find.

Crow tied one end to a tree.

She looped the other end and
placed it on the ground.

The cheese was harder to find.

Crow put the cheese

inside the loop of string.

She hid the string under leaves.

Now all she needed

was a good smell.

But that was the hardest part.

Crow could not carry a smell.

19

She saw some fish frying
in a pan over a fire.
But that was not a smell
she could carry.

She saw a skunk

spraying her perfume.

Crow could carry that smell,

but she did not want to!

She flew away fast.

Then Crow found
a very good smell.
She spied three bowls of stew.
The smell of stew
would be perfect
for Crow's plan.
But she could not carry a bowl.

"The only way to carry stew,"

Crow thought,

"is to wear it."

The stew in the big bowl
was too hot.

The stew in the middle bowl
was too cold.

The stew in the little bowl
was just right.
Crow could wear that stew.
She poured it right over her head.
It ran all over her feathers.

Crow flew past Fox's den.

The good smell flew with her.

Fox sniffed.

The smell made

his mouth water.

Fox came out of his den.

Crow flew from tree to tree,

leading him along.

Fox did not see her.

He was following the good smell.

Crow led Fox to the cheese
and the hidden loop of string.
When Fox saw cheese
instead of stew,
he was surprised.

But Fox liked cheese even better

than he liked stew.

He could not wait to gobble it up.

Crow pulled on the string.

The loop closed tight around Fox's paw.

He was trapped!

Crow flew down
and Fox flew up.
Fox yelled.
Crow laughed and laughed.
Fox dropped the cheese
right into Crow's open beak.

"Delicious!"

she said.

"Thank you, Fox,

for that tasty snack.

I do love a nice bit of cheese."

Fox shook his paw in the air.

"I'll get even with you, Crow!"

he shouted.

"No one outfoxes a fox!"

That was the second fight.

The third fight was even worse.

Chapter 3

Revenge Is a Dish
Best Served with Cheese

Fox fumed.

He did not like flying up

in the air.

He did not like losing.

He did not like Crow.

He plotted a way to get even
with her.
For his plan,
he needed three things—
a scarecrow,
a piece of cheese,
and a birdcage.

Step one was easy.

There was a scarecrow

in the cornfield.

Step two was a little harder.

He did not know where Crow kept

finding all that cheese!

He looked in burrows

and nests

and dens.

Finally he found

a nice piece of cheese

in a little cabin.

Fox found some wood
and built a cage.
Fox's plan was perfect.

He went to the cornfield.
He hid the birdcage
in a haystack.

He hid himself
in the scarecrow's clothes.
He held out the cheese
and waited.

Soon, along came Crow.

She spotted the cheese

in the scarecrow's hand.

Crow landed

on the scarecrow's hand.

Just as she took the cheese

in her beak,

the scarecrow's hand closed

on her leg.

"I've got you now, Crow.

I told you I would get even

with you!"

cried Fox.

Crow could not get away.

Fox shoved Crow
into the birdcage
and locked it tight.
He grabbed the cheese
from Crow's beak.

He was about to gobble it up
when a net fell over
both Fox and Crow.
"Help!" yelled Fox.
"Help!" yelled Crow.

"I've got you now,

Fox and Crow!"

said Mama Bear.

"That will teach you

not to steal my cheese."

Fox and Crow looked

at each other.

They were both sly.

They were both smart.

But they were not as sly or smart

as Mama Bear.

Fox and Crow are still enemies.

But now they do not fight
each other.

They have to work together,

making cheese for Mama Bear.